RETURN OF THE SHADOWS

NORMA FARBER

Illustrations by Andrea Baruffi

A Laura Geringer Book

An Imprint of HarperCollins*Publishers*

Return of the Shadows
Text copyright © 1992 by Thomas Farber
Illustrations copyright © 1992 by Andrea Baruffi
Printed in the U.S.A. All rights reserved.
Typography by Al Cetta
1 2 3 4 5 6 7 8 9 10
First Edition

Library of Congress Cataloging-in-Publication Data
Farber, Norma.
    Return of the shadows / Norma Farber ; illustrations by Andrea
Baruffi.
      p.   cm.
    "A Laura Geringer book."
    Summary: Shadows rebel and run free, finding themselves
mismatched—palmtree-shadows with joggers, camel-shadows
with icebergs, frog-shadows with skiers—until, longing for their
familiar forms, they return home.
    ISBN 0-06-020518-0.—ISBN 0-06-020519-9 (lib. bdg.)
    [1. Shadows—Fiction.]   I. Baruffi, Andrea, ill.   II. Title.
PZ7.F2228Re   1992   91-27517
[E]—dc20   CIP
                                               AC

To the memory of Norma Farber
and her love affair with the English language.
—E.F.S., S.B.F., T.D.F., M.F.

To my good friend Laura
—A.B.

Once upon a night, just before the blackness lifted, something shivered invisibly. It was the waiting shadow of a sleeping girl named Mimi. The shadow rose, shook itself like a damp cloth, and hissed in a shadowy voice to all the other shadows of the world: "Psst! Let's run free!"

So exactly at daybreak, on the morning of Mimi's shadow's call to freedom, all the shadows tore loose from their moorings and began to roam around the world.

A camel shadow paused to rest under an iceberg.

A rhinoceros shadow leaned against the Washington Monument.

A skyscraper shadow crept into the jungle and mingled with the monkeys.

A bicycle shadow rose to the top of clouds beside an airplane.

And Mimi's shadow scalloped the space alongside a flying dolphin.

The sun grew stronger and brighter.

"Psst!" whispered Mimi's shadow, in a shadow hiss heard around the world. "Why didn't we think of this before?"

"How brave we are!" the others agreed. "We'll never go back."

A palm tree shadow kept pace with a jogger.

Three smokestack shadows fumed on a sand dune in the middle of the Sahara.

Mimi's shadow flitted to a race course and ran beside the winning horse.

The shadows wandered all morning over the face of the world, growing always a little smaller, shrinking bit by bit.

And then there was High Noon, when they noticed they'd disappeared entirely, as usual—but this time without anything familiar to hide under.

But after Noon, the shadows began to spill out again, only on the other side of things, leaning east instead of west.

They grew longer and longer, and bolder and bolder, as the afternoon wore on.

A pair of frog shadows followed a skier down a mountain.

A bridge shadow stretched like a tar path across a World Series baseball game.

And Mimi discovered, as she was playing hopscotch,
that the shadow of an astronaut was hopping beside her.

The shadow world kept stretching eastward, longer and longer and longer until there came a time toward dusk when even Mimi's shadow felt strange—a time when shadows began to fade.

The sunlight was at last quite dim, cut off by the bladelike edge of the horizon; the shadows groped blindly, sinking, sinking and no longer sure of what they were, or if they would ever find themselves again. The black night bumped against them, tripping them, and they became lost. They longed for the known places they had come from: where a shadow recognized its own shape and where, in the hold of darkness, each could cling to the rock or pole or pigeon it lived with for comfort. They began to cry and blamed Mimi's shadow for leading them away from home.

And Mimi's shadow cried, too—"Mimi, Mimi, where are you?"

It was a terrible time in the no place of shadows.

So when the sun first climbed over the lowest flat of land, all the shadows raced to find the places where they had been born. And they arranged themselves, once again, close to each magnificent shape in the world.

Mimi's shadow returned, too, and stayed happily
ever after with Mimi.